Jesse Bear,
What Will You Wear?

Y0-BDC-867

Jesse Bear,
What Will You Wear?

by Nancy White Carlstrom
illustrations by Bruce Degen

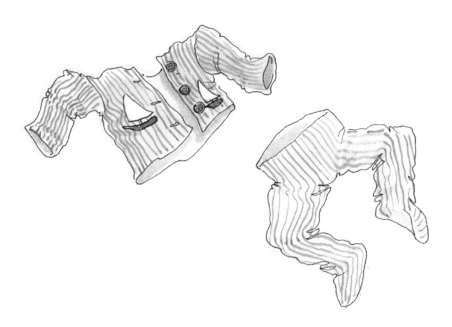

HARCOURT BRACE & COMPANY
Orlando Atlanta Austin Boston San Francisco Chicago Dallas New York
Toronto London

This edition is published by special arrangement with Simon & Schuster Books
for Young Readers, Simon & Schuster Children's Publishing Division.

Grateful acknowledgment is made to Simon & Schuster Books
for Young Readers, Simon & Schuster Children's Publishing Division
for permission to reprint Jesse Bear, What Will You Wear?
by Nancy White Carlstrom, illustrated by Bruce Degen.
Text copyright © 1986 by Nancy White Carlstrom;
illustrations copyright © 1986 by Bruce Degen.

Printed in the United States of America

ISBN 0-15-307279-2

3 4 5 6 7 8 9 10   026   99 98 97

To Jesse David,
   the real Jesse Bear,
   with love
        – N.W.C.

For Denny, Lisa, and Brian
        – B.D.

Jesse Bear, what will you wear?
What will you wear in the morning?

My shirt of red
Pulled over my head
Over my head in the morning.

I'll wear my pants
My pants that dance
My pants that dance in the morning.

I'll wear a rose
Between my toes
A rose in my toes in the morning.

I'll wear the sun
On my legs that run
Sun on the run in the morning.

I'll wear the sand
On my arm and hand
Sand on my hand in the morning.

Jesse Bear, what will you wear
What will you wear at noon?

I'll wear my chair.
You'll wear your chair?

I'll wear my chair
'Cause I'm stuck there
Stuck in my chair at noon.

I'll wear carrots and peas
And a little more please

Celery crunch
And sprouts in a bunch

An apple to bite
And a moustache of white

Juice from a pear
And rice in my hair
That's what I'll wear at noon.

Jesse Bear, what will you wear
What will you wear at night?

Not my shirt
It's covered with dirt
Not my pants
That sat in the ants
Ants in my pants tonight.

Jesse Bare, what will you wear
What will you wear at night?
Water to float
My bubbles and boat
I'll wear in the tub tonight.

My pj's with feet
And face on the seat

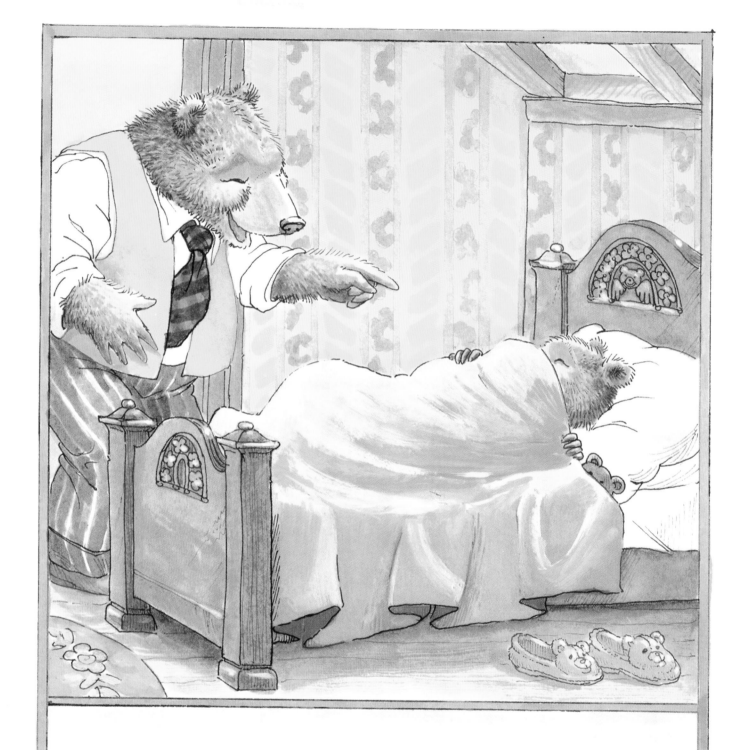

My blanket that's blue
And plays peek-a-boo

Bear hugs from you
And three kisses too
That's what I'll wear tonight.

Jesse Bear, what will you wear
What will you wear at night?

Sleep in my eyes
And stars in the skies
Moon on my bed
And dreams in my head
That's what I'll wear tonight.